EASTERINE KIRE is a poet, novelist, short-story writer and a writer of children's books. Her first novel, *A Naga Village Remembered* (reissued as *Sky Is My Father*), was also the first Naga novel to be published in English. Her other novels include *Son of the Thundercloud* (winner of the Bal Sahitya Puraskar 2018 and the Tata Literature Live! Book of the Year Award 2017); *Bitter Wormwood* (shortlisted for The Hindu Prize 2013); and *When the River Sleeps* (winner of the Hindu Prize 2015). Easterine Kire's work has been translated into German, Croatian, Uzbek, Norwegian and Nepali. In 2011 she was awarded the governor's medal for excellence in Naga literature.

Don't Run, My Love

Easterine Kire

SPEAKING TIGER

SPEAKING TIGER BOOKS LLP
125 A, Shahpur Jat, Near Asiad Village
New Delhi–110049, India

First published in paperback by Speaking Tiger 2017

ISBN: 978-93-87164-03-1
eISBN: 978-93-87164-04-8

10 9 8 7 6 5 4 3

Typeset in Sabon Roman by SÜRYA, New Delhi
Printed at Sanat Printers, New Delhi

Don’t Run, My Love

ANYONE WHO SET EYES ON HIM, MAN OR WOMAN, young or old, had to admit that he was a beautiful creature indeed, the young man who called himself Kevi and who walked into the lives of the two women at harvest time.

They were struggling with a particularly heavy load of newly threshed paddy when he appeared, and insisted on helping them carry it.

'Oh, this is embarrassing,' Visenuo protested. She and her daughter, Atuonuo, were busy hauling sacks of paddy to the shed at the top of the field. Some weeks ago, the water in the terraces had dried up as the stalks of paddy stood in the sun and ripened in golden sheaves. The harvest in the village had been delayed by a week because the *liedepfu*, the ritual initiator of the harvest, had lain sick in her bed for a week. Precious days had been lost and now the race against time and the elements had begun to bring in the harvest before unseasonal rain came and destroyed the hard work of several months. The two women did not expect any help from their neighbours because everyone was busy working to get their own harvests to safety. Nearly one third of the previous year's harvest had been spoiled by rain that had pelted down mercilessly on the final day as they were beating the sheaves of paddy to separate the grains from the stalks. Since it was taboo to throw away grain, they had brought it all inside, but the grain turned black within weeks and had to be used for chicken feed.

'We will split the paddy into smaller sacks,' Visenuo explained to the stranger by way of refusing his offer of help.

'There's no time for that,' the young man said with urgency in his tone. 'Look how overcast the sky is. It will rain soon. Let me carry the paddy to the shed. Better not risk getting it soaked.'

Visenuo had to agree with his reasoning, and reluctantly let go of her hold on the sack.

'You two can bring the others,' he shouted as he hurried to the hut with the load of grain.

'Azuo, who is he?' Atuonuo asked in surprise.

Visenuo shook her head and said, 'I have no idea, but let's find out later. Look, he was right about the rain. It's almost here!' Hurriedly, they dragged the sacks to the shelter of the hut, and the stranger went back for the paddy remaining in the fields.

When every sack was safely inside, he turned around and introduced himself.

'My name is Kevi. I happened to be passing by this way when I saw you struggling with that big load.'

'Well thank you so much, Kevi. It was our good fortune that you came by just then. I am Visenuo, and this is my daughter Atuonuo. We lost quite a bit of grain last year, so we are relieved to have got the harvest to safety now.'

'Then it's good we got it to the hut in time. If you don't need any more help, I should get going,' the young man said and stepped towards the door.

'No, of course not. You must stay and share our food. That is the least we can offer you.' They both insisted that he stay back. Offering a meal was the traditional way to thank somebody who had given unsolicited help.

'In any case,' added Visenuo, 'this rain looks like it will fall all afternoon. Just listen to that thunder! It's dangerous to be out in that. It's a proper storm building up.'

'You're right,' Kevi said looking out the window. The wind was bending the trees over, and big drops of rain splashed on the dry ground. Everything was dry as it had not rained for months, and, in a little while, the heavy rain began to drench the dried grass, and small pools of water formed in the fields.

'I guess it is going to take its own time to clear up.' Kevi remarked as he took the lone chair in the room.

'Looks like it,' Visenuo answered with a smile. 'Now I will get the fire going and we can all eat. Tuonuo, will you bring some more wood?'

Atuonuo quickly looked away from the young man to her mother. She mumbled a yes and went to collect wood from the corner. She blushed in embarrassment when she realized she had been staring at the young man. Her hair had fallen forward and framed her delicate features and dark eyes. At eighteen, Atuonuo was almost as strong as her mother. She had reached the age of marriage. In fact, her grand-aunt thought she was in danger of being passed over, because girls younger than her were already married and had borne children. But Atuonuo would not entertain the thought of marrying yet. A couple of young men had proposed, but she had refused both of them. That was the custom amongst her people: young men proposed to girl after girl and married the one who said yes. So a girl had the right to refuse if she didn't like a suitor.

Atuonuo's father had died when she was only seven, and her mother had never remarried. Together, the two of them worked their fields, and much of their time was spent in work. In the first months of each new year, they hired workers to help with the ploughing, breaking up hard clods of earth, and coaxing the soil to be more malleable for the seeds that would be sown after the rain had softened the earth. The early rain in the months of March and April was used for planting beans, pumpkins and any vegetable belonging to the gourd family. But work began in earnest only when the monsoon rains came to the ancient green valley, and farmers could flood their fields with sufficient water to plant rice. Harvest time made all their hard work worthwhile and no one missed a day's work then.

From the dark corner where the wood was stacked, Atuonuo stole glances at the stranger. He was tall and lean, and had a very pleasing face that drew one in and kept one's attention riveted. He was much better looking than any of the men back in the village. And he was so self-assured; it was all rather fascinating to her. He gazed in her direction, and she shyly turned her attention to the wood and brought it to her mother.

Soon, Visenuo had a big fire going. The room warmed up considerably, and it was a welcome heat in the winter months. The heat brought out the scent of new paddy. It was a sweet and strong smell—like sunshine trapped between husk and grain.

'So Kevi, you live around these parts?' Visenuo asked.

'Not really. My house is a day's walk away. I am a trapper and a hunter; I am travelling to meet a friend in the next village. Actually, I was taking a shortcut through your fields when I saw the two of you.'

'How fortunate for us that you did!' Visenuo said. Atuonuo busied herself with adding more wood to the fire. When she saw that the food was warmed and ready to be served, she brought out three plates and kept them ready. Visenuo began to ladle out rice and broth into the plates.

'Give that to Kevi,' she instructed her daughter. Atuonuo took the heaped plate of food to the young man.

He laughed and protested, 'If I eat all of that, what will be left for you two?'

'We have enough,' Atuonuo replied. 'Azuo always makes a lot of food during harvest time. Please eat.'

'And so I do,' Visenuo agreed. 'We sometimes don't finish until late at night, and then it is good to have cooked food ready so we don't have to take the trouble again.'

'Women are so wise,' Kevi said with a smile as he accepted the food from Atuonuo. 'I lost my mother at birth so I never knew a mother's love. My father brought me up on his own.'

Both women made sympathetic noises but he stopped them. 'That's all in the past. I don't feel sorry for myself anymore.'

They finished their food with little conversation. It was raining heavily now, and they had to shout over the noise of the rain in order to be heard. Fortunately, the violence with which the storm broke meant that its energies were soon depleted. As the rain eased off, they could see the sun breaking through, and the water on the ground evaporated and drifted upwards in veils of mist.

'NOW I SHOULD DEFINITELY GO,' KEVI DECLARED and got up from his seat. 'Thank you for the excellent meal.'

'*We* should thank you for your help. We are so gratcful.'

'It's nothing. Any other man would have done the same.' He picked up his bag and went out the door. At the gate he turned and waved at them, and was soon hidden by the bamboo grove.

'What a good-looking young man! I haven't seen such a handsome face in all my years,' Visenuo remarked.

'He looks like a girl,' Atuonuo answered with a wry smile.

'Not really,' Visenuo countered. 'His features are

more feminine than other men, but he is what one would call very handsome.'

'Yes he is handsome. And he was helpful,' she reluctantly agreed. What Atuonuo did notice was that he was very different from the young men of her age. When he sat with her mother he listened to her very attentively and answered her questions politely. Her male age-mates were still quite immature; they only talked about manly sports like wrestling or narrated stories of hunts they had heard on the nights they spent in the *kichuki,* the male dormitory. She didn't care for the boys of her age who teased her and hid her things when they went out together on herb-gathering days. If she got married, it would have to be to an older man.

Her mother stood by the open door and looked upwards. The skies were clearing and though there were a few rain clouds in the distance, another downpour was unlikely.

'We should go home with one load each. We can come back tomorrow if the weather holds out.'

'All right, Azuo.' They chose their loads carefully. If the bag felt light when they set out, they both knew that as they walked on, the loads would get heavier and heavier until they felt as if their heads were going to burst. They used the *kephou*, a sturdy woven band which can be used for carrying both baskets and grain bags. One end of the band is placed under the bottom of the bag and tied in a firm knot. The other end, which is the wider bit, rests on the carrier's head. In this way, the farmers spent many days carrying the produce of their farms to the village after the harvest.

Visenuo lifted her load onto the wooden seat that Kevi had vacated. Next, she helped her daughter with her load. She then knelt down, put the *kephou* on her head, and leaned forward slightly before heaving up on to her feet. She adjusted the load so that it rode a little higher and exerted less pressure on her lower back.

They walked out of the hut, pulled the door shut, and latched it. No one would steal their grain, but wild animals could break in if they didn't hear the sounds of humans for long. They went through the little gate, shut it, and walked past the grove of creaking bamboos. The grass was still wet, but the sun was shining fiercely, and after a while they were sweating.

'Do you need to rest?' Visenuo asked.

'No. Let's make it to the fig tree as soon as possible,' Atuonuo urged her mother.

This was no time for conversation. They each struggled onwards with their loads, and the only sounds were the heavy breathing of the women, interspersed by a bird's twittering and the scratchy noises made by squirrels scampering in the bushes. Theirs was the last field, some distance away from the others'. This was why they needed to spend more nights in the hut there than the others whose farmland lay closer to the village. During raintime their neighbours were used to the two not coming back to the village for up to a week; they would be spending nights at the hut to finish the work of transplanting paddy. This was how they cut down on time wasted walking back and forth to the village, and it helped them focus on work in the fields for days on end. This was how they managed to farm even in the absence of a man to help with the toughest jobs.

It was a hard life but it was the only one they knew. In the village, widows and their children had very few options. One could not give up working in the fields. There was no extra grain to be bought from the other villagers. Even if there was, where would they find the money to buy it? So they never stopped to think of another life. There had been a couple of women in the next village who had gone away to start shops in town selling herbs, and whatever vegetables the villagers could supply them, but the place they called town was crowded and dirty. Then there were those places where women sat in dingy little rooms with a few tables and benches, selling home-brewed wine to loud-mouthed men. That was not the kind of life Visenuo wanted to give her daughter. So, even if the labour was hard, they lived on in the village, working the land the only way they knew.

The old fig tree stood ahead of them in a pleasant clearing. Grunting, they squatted and shrugged off their loads at its base. The two sat on its moss-covered roots, wiped the sweat off their faces, and rested. Behind the fig tree, the forest took over and, in the early hours, field-goers could hear deer barking. But at the tree, the villagers had set up stones for weary travellers, and it had become a resting point on this route.

'We can't afford to wait here. It's later than I thought. That rain stole a few hours of our time,' Visenuo said, looking around her.

'You're right Azuo, the sun is already red. It's beginning to set.' Atuonuo was alarmed.

They usually avoided being on the path so late in the evening. They had heard too many stories of spirits waylaying field-goers on their way home.

'Come, we must hurry then,' Visenuo answered quickly. She put the strap of the *kephou* on her forehead and heaved the load of paddy up. She then assisted Atuonuo and the two resumed their walking. The rest had refreshed them and they quickened their pace, trying to cover as much ground as possible before the light went. They fell back into their customary silence, and each one kept to herself the anxiety over being caught outdoors in the dark. They had come to the fields of the other villagers, but all were deserted. The thought that they were probably the only ones about made them uneasy. However, both of them avoided voicing it.

Thankfully, they were coming to the last leg of their walk home. The long line of trees on either side of them had grown thinner, and the path they were on would soon join that which led to the village. When they reached the junction, they looked back but saw nothing. The trees were motionless, and the fields were very distant now. They were both relieved that they had completed their journey without encountering any wild animals or spirits.

Mother and daughter both hurriedly entered through the village gate and turned left to take the path that led home. They were eased by the human sounds in the village. An old man coughing, a woman scolding her children, pots being stirred and fires stoked. In the *kichukis*, the young men were talking loudly after having started off on the homebrew early. Even this they found familiar and comforting.

Atuonuo, who had been in the lead, opened the door to their house and quickly lowered her load onto a chair so she could help her mother.

THEY HAD BEEN AWAY FOR FIVE DAYS THIS HARVEST time. A musty smell lingered in the air, and though the house was dark, Atuonuo knew her way about well. She deftly felt for and found the matchbox, lit the kerosene lamp, and lighted up the kitchen. It was quite cold inside.

'I'll get a fire going,' she said and began to pile up bamboo shavings and slivers of wood in the hearth. The matches were a little damp but she finally managed to spark a tiny flame. She carefully fed the flame with slices of dry bamboo and twigs. The fire grew until she felt confident about placing bigger pieces of wood over the flame.

'Fill up the kettle and heat it,' her mother instructed. 'We will need to eat before we go to bed.'

They then made a quick meal for the night, tossing dried meat and dried mustard leaves into a pot in which a little rice was simmering. The broth boiled over, and the cooks soon declared it done. Visenuo ladled the food into their plates.

'Tuonuo, you are so good at making a fire,' her mother complimented her daughter. 'Your grandfather used to say that a house needs a fire. The smoke from the fire strengthens the walls and helps it stay in place for a longer time. When a house is abandoned, it falls apart very soon. *The house was missing its owner*, that is what we say when that happens.'

'You know so many things Azuo,' Atuonuo said. 'I wish I knew half the things you do.'

'Well, I only know the things that the village has taught me from childhood, and I try to pass them on to you. Do you know that some people are called *thehou nuo*?'

'What does that mean?'

'Since the *thehou* is the communal house where men spend their nights, *thehou nuo* means child of the *thehou*. The boys who have been brought up in that tradition learn things about our culture. They use it to guide them through life, and when people see them behaving in a certain way, people refer to them as *thehou nuo*. A girl can also earn such a title when people see that she knows the ways of the village.'

'Then I hope I will become one too. Will it stop me being scared of spirits and dark places?' They both laughed.

'The *thehou* cannot help you to stop fearing the unknown. But it can teach you to be brave. After every victory in battle we celebrate the courage of the warriors of our village. That doesn't mean they fear nothing. They are humans too, and naturally they have their fears. But the *thehou* teaches them to set their fears aside when they go into battle. Their enemies are also equipped in the same way. That is why we call the victors the bravest of the brave. They are the ones who have learned to ignore their fears completely.'

'Well if that is the case, I'll never make a good warrior,' Atuonuo stated. 'I can't help feeling scared of being out in the forest after dark like we were this evening. I don't like it when we have to sleep in the field hut, but at least when we do, it helps that we always have a fire burning.'

'I understand. Things are strange in the darkness. It is as though the dark becomes a world of its own. The animals of the forest come out on seeing that people are no longer around, and they can be quite menacing.'

They had finished eating by now and Atuonuo took her mother's plate away. She washed the plates and pots with hot water, which made it easier to for her to scrape the food off. She filled up the kettle again and replaced it on the fire.

'For your bath,' she said to her mother as she went to fetch the bucket. The outhouse was not far from the main house. Like the other outhouses in the village, it had a sack covering the entrance.

After they had both bathed, they continued to sit by the fire sipping black tea. It was a routine they followed after dinner. The last thing they did before going to bed was to bury a firebrand in the warm ash so they would have no trouble starting the fire in the morning.

'We had better get some sleep,' Visenuo said, getting up from her chair and stretching. 'We will have to make several trips to bring in the harvest.'

'All right, Azuo. We can at least start early tomorrow and be back home before dark.'

They slept easily, the deep slumber of the farmer who exhausts her body all day in physical labour and is rewarded with heavy sleep at night.

Morning came with the crowing of the village roosters. At first cockcrow, Visenuo turned over and slept again. Their fields were too far to make two trips back and forth in one day. It was better to rest well and make the one trip each day until they had transported the whole harvest.

By the time they started, the sun had come out and the ground was dry. Had they left an hour earlier, they would have seen dew on the grass. Cold weather had set in; the elders always took care to see that harvest was begun before the frost. Frost would ruin the harvest as surely as rain would if it was left too late in the fields.

They were walking along the track that was so familiar to both of them, a path they traversed more than a hundred times in a year. That fact had not made it easier as the years went by. Carrying the harvest home over the long distance was still, for them, the hardest part of field work. When they were at the hut, Atuonuo, who had reached first, called out, 'Azuo, someone has left us meat!'

This was unexpected. Visenuo hurried to the hut and saw the leg of a deer that had been hung on their door with a length of twine.

'Goodness! Someone has been lucky at hunting! Do we know who it could be?' Visenuo wondered. The meat was fresh and bloody.

'Azuo, this is so much meat! We have never had anyone give us a whole leg before!'

'That's true. We have to find out who our benefactor is and try to compensate him somehow.'

They cut down the meat and took it inside the hut. Visenuo made a fire and began to burn the skin. Atuonuo protested but Visenuo answered, 'If I don't do this now, the meat will go bad. Even if we feel the gift is too generous, that's no reason for us to let good meat go waste.' She continued to cut off the meat and burn the skin and clean it with a knife. Eventually Atuonuo joined her, muttering, 'I wish we knew who the giver was.'

THE DAY PASSED QUICKLY. CLEANING THE MEAT HAD taken them longer than they expected, and now they had no time to waste in starting back for the village. They ate quickly and packed the meat to take along. They then hoisted their loads and prepared to set out, having latched the door. All of a sudden Atuonuo stopped and said, 'Azuo, why not leave something for him in case he should come back? To show we appreciate the gift?'

'That's a good idea, but what can we leave, and where?'

'The vegetables you picked, the gourd and pumpkin! We have enough vegetables in the house. We can leave those for him!' she said excitedly.

'What a good idea! I'll hang them here over the

door so he will know they're for him. If they are still there tomorrow, we will take them home with us.'

They started for home with the sun still high in the sky, and when they reached the boundary between the fields, they met one of their neighbours.

'Visenuo, Tuonuo, you've finished harvesting, then?' Vilhu asked when they met at the crossing.

'Yes, and you?' Visenuo asked.

'Oh yes. We should be through with carrying back the last loads by tomorrow. I'm mending one of the fences today. Do you need help this week? I can help for a couple of days,' he offered. The widows in the village often received help from the others by way of a few days' free labour. Visenuo was grateful for Vilhu's offer but did not want to risk displeasing his wife. She had once pointed out that Vilhu was more eager to help the widow than do his share of the work. So she refused Vilhu's offer politely, saying that they had also finished their lot, and it was just a few more days of transporting left. She told Vilhu she would gladly ask for help if she needed it.

'You be sure to do that, Visenuo. You shouldn't have to suffer because your man's gone early. What would we be if we cannot help one another?' Vilhu was a good man, and Visenuo wished she could accept help from him without being nervous about offending his wife. He was not the sort to want a favour back; he was just a very helpful and generous person.

After their little exchange, the two women went on their way and Vilhu went back to repairing the fence around his field. Crossing the line of trees, they came within sight of the village. The sun was low on the horizon, and they could see smoke drifting upward from the houses—people were already cooking their evening meal. Happy that they would reach their destination before dark, they continued on the path and soon entered the village gate.

Their village had two names. The first settlers called it Phesa, new village. After a few years they renamed it Kija, village of the blessed house. No one used the old name anymore. As they came in, they saw some people out on the *dahou,* the circular sitting place at the entrance to the village. The hard stone seats were shiny from constant use. The small assembly of people called out greetings to which the women gave the appropriate response. Most of the company were men sitting with their tall horns of brew, watching the field-goers coming home.

A number of young mothers were also standing at the *dahou,* which was also a popular viewing point as it offered a panoramic view of the fields in the horizon. Carrying their babies on their backs with the straps tied in front, they walked back and forth on the elevated platform softly singing lullabies. The children showed no signs of sleepiness. They peeped out from behind their mothers' backs, curiously scrutinizing every movement around them. These men and women would return home and inform their families how late or early the harvesters had come home, and if they thought they were carrying heavy or medium loads. It was just the kind of small talk that was common when a community lived at such close quarters.

Visenuo and Atuonuo turned left and were soon home. They went into the first room, and lowered their loads before shutting the door.

'Ah, at least we can have meat tonight,' Visenuo said.

'Yes. Though we have no idea where it's come from,' Atuonuo responded in a lukewarm voice.

'So what? It's good meat. You will relish it once I have cooked it.'

'I don't know. I can't help feeling a bit uneasy about it. If we could have thanked the hunter, I would have had no qualms about cooking and eating it. But this way, I feel as though we are about to eat stolen food.'

'What an idea! It was gifted to us. It wouldn't be left there on our door if it was not a gift.' Visenuo sounded irritated.

'Sorry Azuo, you are right. I'll get the fire going now.'

The meat was cut up into smaller pieces, mixed with dried red chilli, and left to simmer in a little water. They used an earthen pot; they always cooked meat in an earthen pot. Atuonuo carefully brought the pot to the fire. It had belonged to her grandmother and there was a small crack at the mouth. Nevertheless, Visenuo insisted on using it as meat cooked in an earthen pot tasted far better than meat cooked in an aluminium pot; people would say there was something about mud pots that added a pleasing flavour to the meat. Whatever the reason was, it certainly made the meat very tender.

Atuonuo had dug up some country ginger from their backyard. She thoroughly cleaned off the soil, washed it several times and pounded it for the pot. They grew spices such as basil, chilli, garlic and ginger for their kitchen in the backyard. It was not a regular garden as there wasn't enough space. Weeds had grown unchecked because they had been too busy with the fields. In one corner was a large patch of *japan nha*, Crofton weed. They had not uprooted it because it was said to be effective against malaria and stomach aches. Every household had a small garden space similar to theirs to supply their kitchen needs.

The meat had been simmering for more than an hour when Atuonuo took the lid off and immediately cried out.

'What's the matter?' Visenuo asked.

'The steam burnt my hand!'

'Wait, I'll get a mug of cold water for you.' Visenuo got the water and Atuonuo thrust her hand into it. She felt instant relief when she did that.

'Keep your hand in the water for some time,' her mother ordered, and took over the cooking. 'This pot holds the heat in so well, too well in fact. I should have warned you.'

She added the ginger and tasted the gravy. It needed a little more salt and that was added, the pot thoroughly stirred and taken off the fire.

'Are you ready to eat, my dear?' Visenuo asked solicitously. By then Atuonuo's hand had become much better, and the burning had greatly diminished.

'Yes Azuo, let's eat. I am quite hungry,' she answered. They sat beside the fire on low wooden stools and ate.

'That gravy is so rich in flavour. I may not be able to open my eyes tomorrow,' Visenuo sighed after she had finished eating.

'Why not, Azuo?'

'Well, we say that when you have enjoyed a meal so thoroughly, your eyes become swollen the next day, and everyone can see it, and they can tell you had been feasting the night before.'

After dinner, they lingered by the fire making plans for the following day.

'Azuo, I think I know who left us the meat,' Atuonuo said in a small voice.

'Who, dear?'

'It must have been the young man who helped us the other day. Kevi.'

'Hmm. You are probably right. He did say he was a trapper. Well, I hope he comes by tomorrow or one of these days. It would be nice to see him again.'

'Yes,' Atuonuo replied.

'I thought you didn't like him,' Visenuo said in surprise. 'You were reluctant to say anything nice about him.'

'It was not like that, Azuo. I just felt nervous about what to say to him. You two were doing all the talking, but I felt like a child because I couldn't think of anything to say. But then again, I preferred to watch him from my corner and see what he was really like.'

'Let's see if he will come by again soon. If it was him who brought the meat, it means he likes us.'

They put out the fire and went to bed. Harvest time had its own mechanical routine, and until they had completed the task of bringing the harvest home, they could not start anything new.

'AZUO! SOMEONE HAS LEFT US MEAT AGAIN!' ATUONUO had reached the hut, and was the first to see the gift.

'Really?' Visenuo quickened her steps and came up. She looked at the meat and said, 'Oh this is getting very awkward that we don't know who our benefactor is.'

'It's a big portion! This time we really must find out who it is.' Visenuo removed the meat that was hanging by a piece of twine on the door and took it inside. It was not deer meat this time. Fat covered one side of the hunk.

'Tuonuo, we should sleep here tonight and catch him,' Visenuo said. There seemed to be no other way of finding out. If they told the other villagers about it, they would tease Atuonuo saying she had a secret admirer, which was just what it looked like. Visenuo looked at her daughter and bit her tongue. She didn't want to upset her, but perhaps there was a suitor about who was trying to court her. They would find out more soon, she thought, and kept her thoughts to herself.

However, Atuonuo kept asking about the meat. Why had he left another portion? Could there be some other reason why the meat had been left at their door today? Did her mother have any clue who the giver might be? Did her father have some hunter friends who might be doing this? Atuonuo was a little annoyed that her mother did not know. Finally, Visenuo could not stop herself from blurting out that it was probably the work of a suitor wanting to marry Atuonuo. That abruptly stopped all the questions from the daughter, and the mother was immediately sorry that she had put it so bluntly.

'Tuonuo, I didn't mean to make you worry, but this is the sort of thing a young man does when he likes a girl and would like to marry her. He brings gifts to her on a regular basis and then asks for her hand.'

'So that means this person wants to marry me?' Atuonuo looked dismayed.

'It doesn't necessarily have to mean that. He could be just a friend who wants to give us good food to eat. It could be the work of *Kepenuopfu*. Until we know for sure, we can't say it is this or that. Come, we must not let this keep us from our work. Make a fire; we must prepare that meat or it will go bad.'

Visenuo went to the hearth to make a fire. The dry logs crackled and blazed into life. The women were sitting on low wooden stools.

'That's a fire to be proud of!'

'Kevi! What a surprise!'

'I'm sorry I did not come by yesterday to help you, but here I am today and you may give me any work at all.' He was charming and carefree all at once.

'We have no work for you, young man. But we are so puzzled over who might have left us meat yesterday and today. Could it possibly have been you?'

He hung his head and muttered, 'I'm guilty. It was me.'

'Oh what a relief to hear that. We were wondering which of our acquaintances or friends could have done it. Thank you very much, but this must stop now. We won't know what to do with so much meat!'

'You can dry it and preserve it for the cold months,' Kevi suggested. 'It is good to have a store of dried meat in winter. Keeps you warm.'

'I'll follow your advice but only if you promise not to give us any more meat.' Visenuo looked at him with a stern face, but she couldn't keep it up for long and a little smile escaped her.

'I do it for my friends, and I really don't have many friends.'

'Still,' Visenuo persisted. In the meantime, Atuonuo had filled a mug with cold water and came up to him with it.

'Thank you. You must be tired working so hard every day, Atuonuo?'

'Not really. I am quite used to it. Azuo and I will work a few days more to get the harvest to the village, and then we will have a long rest from field work.' It was the first time she had spoken that many words to him. He was sitting in the chair by the fire, and with the light falling on his face, she saw once more how startlingly handsome he was. No matter how hard she had tried to deny it the first day, she could not hide the fact now that she found him a very attractive young man. Was he really interested in her? Or was her mother grossly mistaken?

It made her dizzy to contemplate that thought; it made her clumsy too, and she dropped the piece of wood she was carrying to the hearth. Bending to pick it up, she tried to collect herself. But if he was not interested, why had he brought them meat twice? It could just be that he saw a mother in Visenuo, she told herself and tried to put the other thing out of her mind.

'You will have to make the fire again, Tuonuo. It's dying. I am going out to take a look at the vegetable patch.' Kevi followed Visenuo out the door and they went to see if there were any gourds ready to be picked.

Whenever they came to the field, Visenuo and Atuonuo took turns making food, and today it was the younger woman's turn. She realized her mother was gently reminding her to get started on the food. Atuonuo cajoled the fire back to life. She got down on her knees and blew at the little embers until the bamboo crackled into life. Slowly she added the twigs and bits of dry leaves and forest debris, and soon she had a good fire going. The rice pot went on top of the fire and was bubbling in no time. This was routine work for her and she went about it almost automatically, refusing to let the presence of the young man distract her from her duties. In a little while, the cooking was done—rice and a portion of the meat Kevi had brought them.

'FOOD'S READY,' SHE CALLED OUT.

'That was fast!' her mother exclaimed. 'Come Kevi, we will all eat together.' He did not protest this time. Visenuo came into the door carrying a medium-sized pumpkin.

'Should I add some of this to your pot?' she asked, but Atuonuo said it was too late to add anything, and she began to serve them as they sat down by the fire.

It was a simple and wholesome meal. They knew the rice and meat would keep them going the whole day.

'I took the vegetables you had left yesterday. I guessed it was for me,' Kevi explained.

'It was for the giver of the meat, and that being you, of course it was for you.'

Visenuo leaned over and ladled more food into Kevi's plate. Before they started eating, she had made him sit in the chair by the fire. It was her chair, but he was not to know that.

Atuonuo noticed that the two of them were getting along very well, and it seemed to her that Visenuo was becoming more and more maternal with Kevi. As for Kevi, he directed most of his questions to Visenuo, even when it was a question about Atuonuo.

As they were finishing their meal, he asked quite out of the blue, 'Does Atuonuo have a sweetheart back in the village?' He was looking at her, but the question was directed at her mother.

Atuonuo was indignant. They were talking about her as though she were not there, or as though she were a child who did not know her own mind. She made a sound that was pure exasperation.

'Why not ask her yourself?' Visenuo replied. 'I don't think she has a sweetheart; I would know if she did. But yes, she certainly has two or three young men who admire her.'

'This is too much!' Atuonuo exclaimed and stormed towards the door. A look of alarm replaced the intense curiosity on Kevi's face and he sprang after her.

Grabbing her by the arm, he said, 'No, please. I

am very sorry. I didn't mean to upset you. Really, I didn't mean it like that.' His other hand, surprisingly heavy and powerful for a slender man, was on her shoulder. 'Please won't you forgive us? I promise we will not talk like that again.'

Atuonuo felt it would be churlish of her to continue sulking, especially when he was so earnest, so she came back, and even managed a little laugh when Kevi's foot slipped on a pebble and he lurched forward. He agilely flung out his hand and grabbed a post to stop himself from falling.

'Oh that was dangerous! Do you punish people you don't like with tricks like that?' he asked with a mock serious face. The air instantly cleared between them, and the three of them were soon talking about how to get their loads ready for the journey back.

'I can take the heavy sack,' Kevi offered. 'I don't believe either of you can manage that one, and it's pointless to repack it when I can easily carry it.' Visenuo hesitated. It was a long way to the village. It would be such an imposition to let him carry the bag that far.

'In any case,' he added, 'I have some work in the next village so I will be travelling that way. You might as well let me help you this once.' That information made the decision easier.

'Oh well, then you may help. But just this time,

mind. We are not used to taking help from others during harvest season and we mustn't get spoiled,' Visenuo stated firmly. Atuonuo was secretly pleased that he would come with them. She chose a medium-heavy sack for herself and checked that the one for her mother was not too heavy either. It would embarrass her if she had to struggle with her own load. In their age group, they were taught that one must not shy away from hard work. The other thing that was shameful was to start a task and not be able to complete it, so she was making sure that their loads would be manageable. And though her mother was not elderly by any standards, Atuonuo felt she should not be allowed to work as hard as before, and she had begun to take over work that her mother did earlier.

Visenuo found an extra *kephou* that Kevi could use. Together, both women lifted the load of grain on his back, making sure that the wide end of the *kephou* was resting on the middle of his head. They had time to rest three or four times by the roadside since they were starting early. The women had divided up the meat and they carried it packed in leaves and tied securely with twine.

These trips back were always slow going; the heavy loads gave them no respite. Conversation was limited as they had to conserve their energies. So they walked uphill in silence, in single file, looking neither to the left nor to the right. When they came to the other fields, they greeted the workers without looking up at them. By the time they finally arrived in Kija, it was evening. The mothers suckling their babies, and the old men with their horns of brew were watching as they entered the gate. Exchanging perfunctory greetings, Visenuo led the way to their house. A low murmur rippled through the crowd gathered at the *dahou*. Who was the stranger? Was he a relative of Visenuo's? He didn't look like one of their young men. Everyone was curious about the stranger helping the widow bring back her harvest, but no one had the answer to the question uppermost in their minds: Was this a suitor for Atuonuo?

The young mothers and the men at the *dahou* who had witnessed the three of them entering the village went back to their homes and discussed this event with their family members. No one had a clue who the young man was. By late evening, the whole village was abuzz with news of the handsome stranger who was helping the widow and her daughter. Two of Visenuo's paternal relatives made it their business to visit them and get acquainted with the stranger.

But they were sorely disappointed. For Kevi had left not long after they came home with their loads of paddy promising to come by soon. He said he would miss the friend he had to meet if he didn't leave right away. Visenuo had made sure to pack some food for him before sending him on his way.

'Viseu.' It was her aunt Abau's voice. She opened the door and two elderly women stood at the door, Abau and her sister Khonuo.

'Ania, what a surprise. What brings you two here so late? Hope it is not bad news.' Visenuo pulled out chairs for them to sit on.

'It is not bad news from our side,' Abau began, 'but the whole village is asking us about the young man who carried your paddy home. We could not sit at home any longer and keep saying we know nothing of this business.' Abau sounded upset and disappointed. She was in her seventies and considered it her right to know all that was going on in the lives of her children, her grandchildren and her nephews and nieces and their children, especially when it pertained to the female members.

'Nnia just wants to make sure your reputation is safe,' said Khonuo in a softer tone. 'A man visiting a widow is always a matter of great interest for the villagers, especially when you have an eligible daughter in the house.' Visenuo suppressed her irritation. It was times like these that always made her question the wisdom of living in a close-knit community where one was answerable to everyone else for any actions or decisions.

'Ania,' she addressed the older woman, 'that young man made our acquaintance some days ago back at our field hut. He helped us carry a very heavy sack of paddy just before the storm came. We are indebted to him. Today he said he was passing through Kija and offered to carry one of our loads. I didn't stop to think if it might be considered an immoral action if he was allowed to help us. I have given him food in return for his kindness.' Visenuo's irritation was only thinly veiled.

Abau was immediately contrite.

'Viseü, you must not take it the wrong way. You are a young widow and you have a daughter who is of a marriageable age. Well, she is more than that since there are girls her age who are already wives and mothers. If there is any talk linking the two of you with a man, it will not be good for Tuonuo's marriage chances. That was our only concern.'

'He was not trying to marry either of us!' Visenuo retorted sharply.

'Viseu, this is what gets you into trouble time and again. You live in a community. You must heed the rules of the community or risk being talked about by the members of society,' Khonuo was speaking gently. The two of them always did that. When Abau's sharp tongue had angered a relative, Khonuo would soften the blow.

'I don't see what could be so wrong about a kind stranger wanting to help us with loads that a man is meant to carry.' Visenuo refused to back down.

'She is so stubborn, that one.' Abau was still annoyed when they left Visenuo's house. They had come away without getting any information about the stranger: his name, his father's name or the village he hailed from. 'When our nephew married her, even her own mother warned him he would have a tough time taming her. It looks like he didn't succeed.'

'But what could go so wrong, Abau? Maybe this nice young man will marry Tuonuo and take her off her mother's hands. Then you can stop worrying about it getting too late for any man to marry her. In our day, people got married much earlier, but that is changing with today's young people. These days some of them want to wait, and there's nothing wrong with that according to me. Nothing wrong with them wanting to be sure they marry the right one.'

'I don't like to argue with people who are half as stubborn as I am. It tires me. I am too old for this sort of thing, these confrontations. It's like going into battle.'

'I'm sure it's not as bad as that. She is family after all.'

'She is family by marriage, not by blood. Those types are the most difficult to convince that they must protect the family name.'

'Oh Abau, you have to remember the villagers make so much of nothing. If a man is seen talking to a maiden, the next news that flies around is that the two are going to get married! Viseü was probably right to get offended.'

They headed home knowing there was no end to this argument. Only when something did happen, possibly a marriage or the young man's total disappearance from the lives of the two women, would the argument end and another take its place.

VISENUO WAS FATIGUED BY THE ALTERCATION WITH Abau and her sister.

'I'll make tea,' Atuonuo suggested. 'You go and sit down. You've done enough work for one day.'

'Thank you, Tuonuo.'

The fire had died down. Atuonuo used the bamboo shavings to tease the few embers that looked promising. The smoke that drifted up got into her eyes and she was coughing and teary eyed. Refusing to accept defeat, she blew hard on the shavings and, with a loud *boof!*, the flames sprang to life.

'Oh, must the fire too be so hard to make tonight?' Visenuo said in a tired voice.

'Poor you, Azuo. All that trouble with Atsa Abau

over nothing.' Atuonuo handed her a mug of tea and sat down opposite her.

'I always tell myself I have got better at this, but every time she comes, I get very annoyed and end up speaking sharply.' Visenuo's tone was contrite.

'She won't change. Atsa Abau is not the sort to change. What she thinks reflects what the village thinks. Didn't you tell me their family was once the most powerful in the village? And we are part of that family, aren't we? Perhaps that is why she is so anxious that we should not do anything to spoil the family name.'

'Yes, and she thinks we are the only ones capable of doing that! Your grandfather was the wealthiest man in the village. He and his wife hosted four feasts of merit. Invitations were sent out to his friends in all the neighbouring villages. So you see, they were feeding not just their own villagers but people from far and wide. Can you imagine how much food that would involve? Nobody does that sort of thing nowadays because no one is able to till that much food anymore.

'I suspect your grandfather was an arrogant man. My mother hinted at it when I was young. He died on the last night of the fourth feast of merit. They had given a feast for the whole village of about five hundred people. Ntsa Abau and Ntsa Khonuo inherited nothing from his vast wealth. They were his sisters but since they were not male relatives, they could not get any of his property.

'Your father was his sole heir and he was a good provider who always looked after his widowed mother. He made sure his aunts were provided for as well. Then we met and married and you came along. We were so happy. Ntsa Abau urged us to host a feast of merit. She said it was to ensure that your grandfather's name would live on. We both refused. We had only just started our lives together; we had no accumulated grain of our own. It didn't seem right to either of us to use up his father's wealth on a feast of merit that neither of us had any interest in. We both agreed that your grandfather's name was in no danger of fading away from people's memories.

'The four monoliths erected after each feast of merit were set up on the way to the fields. People passed them every day when they went to the fields. They rested at the foot of the monoliths and recounted the feasts of Kezharuokuo, using those moments to recall the great man's name. So he had gotten what he wanted: his name continued to be spoken of long after he had gone. But Ania Abau was very angry when we refused to host a feast of merit.

She accused me of turning your father away from his duty to the village, and his duty to his family. My place in her good books has never been restored since then.'

'What did Apuo want?'

'He never wanted to host a feast. We were very young. We wanted to start a life together; that was our focus. The last thing we wanted was to get involved in a big cultural programme in which man and wife would have to observe days of not going to the fields, or not speaking to visitors, or not sleeping in the same bed on specific days—there were so many taboos to be observed. Your father certainly didn't want that.'

'But they blamed you?'

'It was easier for them to blame me. It's always the newcomer's fault if something is not going smoothly in the family. It was easy to say that I changed his mind. After that, Ania Abau threatened me saying that the person who opposes cultural practices will meet with tragedy. And then your father died early. You were only seven.'

'But Apuo died of swamp fever, you said so yourself. He didn't die as a result of the curse, did he?'

'I don't believe he died of a curse. He came back feverish after a night out at the swamp where they had gone hunting. Two of his friends also came down with the same fever; they survived, your father did not.'

'But Atsa Abau chose to blame you for Apuo's death?'

'I guess it was easier for her to focus her grief and rage on a person, and that person happened to be me.'

'Oh Azuo. But what has all this to do with Kevi helping us?'

'I think they want a commitment from him if he is to keep visiting us. He should say that he will marry you. That will make his visits legitimate and protect your reputation in the village.'

'Azuo! We can't possibly tell him that!'

'No, we can't. But that is what your grandmother expects us to do.'

'Don't let him come to the house then. We can manage the harvest all by ourselves!'

'Atuonuo, we cannot live our lives dictated by what other people think and what they decide for us.'

'But Atsa Abau is so unpleasant when she doesn't get her way,' Atuonuo said in a low voice.

'She is. But let's not waste any more time thinking about that. We should finish our harvesting so we can get ready for the Harvest Festival. Just a few days left from tomorrow.'

'Ah that is the time when you are not allowed to eat rice, isn't it Azuo? Why do we do that?'

'Ah yes, the *Kevakete*. But it's only for one day. The mother of the household has to refrain from eating rice; she eats only boiled lentils. Actually, everyone takes part in the ritual: none of the members of the household are allowed to eat before the mother has eaten. All these things are observed for a reason. These rituals transfer blessings upon our harvest. Do you remember; when you were younger, you and your friends were sent to catch frogs from nearby streams?'

'Oh yes. Atsa Khonuo would go with us and tell us to count the frogs carefully and only cook them in even numbers.'

Atuonuo was recollecting the practice of sending children out to catch hibernating frogs. Khonuo would tell them that it was important for their parents to eat those frogs in particular. Since the frogs slept for months without food, they were taken as a symbol that food in the house would last very long. In this way, the Harvest Festival had its own list of taboos, each intended to propitiate the spirits and prevent the destruction of the grain that had been brought into the granaries. For instance, there was a taboo on eating grasshoppers and dragonflies as these were insects that destroyed crops—it would not do to anger them. The feast of the Harvest Festival was not a big one, though. To celebrate it, each household just needed a pot of meat to go with the newly harvested rice.

ON THE LAST DAY OF THE HARVEST, THE WOMEN again found some meat hanging from their door.

Kevi had not come by for some days. Atuonuo tried to hide her pleasure at this sign that he still thought of them.

'Oh this boy! He should just come by without going through all these rituals!' Visenuo exclaimed.

'What rituals, Azuo?' Atuonuo sounded alarmed.

'Oh it's what I told you about before. When a man continually brings gifts to a woman, it is interpreted as his intention to make a proposal of marriage.'

Atuonuo kept quiet. Kevi seemed to be making his intentions rather clear. It was an exciting prospect to think that he liked her well enough to want to marry her. She picked up the water pot and went down to the stream below the hut. Before she dipped her mug into the water, she took a quick look at her reflection. Her long hair fell forward and obstructed her view. She impatiently pushed it away. The surface of the pool reflected a charming face with the same rosy complexion as her mother. 'You have your father's eyes,' Azuo used to tell her. They were the most arresting part of her—clear, intense eyes that clouded over when she was unhappy or confused.

Atuonuo was not as tall as her mother, and she was much more slender. Visenuo's body had thickened; the way it did with women in the village after birthing a child or two. Even though she worked as hard as a man, the slim form of her youth was gone. No one could call her fat, but her body weight made others describe her as a big-boned woman.

Below the hut, Atuonuo scooped water into the mug and washed her face vigorously. If Kevi were to come today, she wanted to make sure she looked her best. That done, she carried water back to the hut.

When she pushed open the door, Kevi was sitting by the fire.

'Kevi! You startled me!' she said as some of the water splashed on the floor. He sprang up apologetically, and tried to help with the water pot in her hand.

'No, it's okay. I didn't expect you, that's all. Did you leave the meat for us?' she asked quickly.

'It's not much. I found a boar in my traps. Wild boar is very healthy meat.'

'Are you always so lucky with your trapping and hunting?' she asked wonderingly.

As the three of them were conversing they heard a shout from outside.

'Anyone here?' the male voice enquired.

'Who is that?' Visenuo asked in surprise. 'It can't be Vilhu. I know he isn't through working in his own fields.' She opened the door of the hut and shouted back, 'Yes we are here!'

It was the woodsman. He had his massive axe slung over his shoulder and stood at the gate.

'Keyo! Come in! I didn't know it was you.' Visenuo gave him such a hearty welcome that he felt it would be rude to not respond to her welcome, but Keyo kept explaining all the while that he was actually on his way to the forest behind their field.

The two men were introduced to each other and the women quickly made more food.

'Kevi? I don't know you, but if you tell me your father's name, I might be able to see if I have ever met him. I know most of the people who live in these hills,' Keyo commented.

'I am the son of Krucha. He is no more.

My mother's name was Vizolenuo but I never knew her.'

'I knew them both,' the woodsman declared. 'They were fine people. I'm sorry for your loss.'

'I like to believe that life's losses are going to make me stronger.' It was the kind of thing that an older person might have said, and it sounded right when they did. Yet when Kevi uttered these words, they somehow did not sound appropriate.

'You must eat with us, Keyo. Everything is ready,' Visenuo extended a warm invitation. The woodsman protested but the other three assured him there was enough food, and it would go to waste if he didn't eat.

'All right then. I don't like to see good food go to waste.' Keyo said this laughingly as he sat down. Visenuo and Atuonuo first served the men. They then took food for themselves and joined the men.

'Do you remember how your father died?' Keyo addressed the question to Kevi.

'No. I was quite young and my aunt wouldn't let me watch when they were washing his body.'

'It was an odd thing. He had been sick for some days and when he died and they were washing his body, they found a wound in his back that had been caused by a spear. But he had not been anywhere in the weeks before his death. I still remember that.'

'Were you at his funeral?' Kevi asked in surprise.

'I was. My uncle took me along, saying that a great man had died and we should honour him by attending his funeral. He was not from my village, you know. But we were in the area so we went.'

'Hmm, that brings up so many memories,' Kevi said thoughtfully.

After eating, Keyo thanked them and went on his way. He was headed south, and promised he would stop by on his way back. And then he was gone, swiftly swallowed by the shadows of trees.

'What does he do?' Kevi asked curiously.

'The woodsman? He is basically an axe for hire. He chops trees for those who have money to hire his skills. And he is a trapper like you. No one knows these areas as well as Keyo does. The men say he has travelled so widely that he is well known in the Zeliang areas as well. I suppose he plies his trade there too.'

'What a useful man to know.' Kevi sounded sincere but Atuonuo noticed that he was smiling as though he were amused. What could there be about the woodsman's life that he found amusing? That thought crossed her mind. But she forgot all about it when he turned towards her and included her in that smile.

THE SUN WAS BEGINNING ITS DESCENT WHEN THEY got ready to leave. Visenuo had decided not to carry the last two loads home, and Kevi's offer to help was also refused. They did not want to feed the gossip mills in the village. If she could not be sure of Kevi's intentions, she was not about to encourage him. Atuonuo would not find any suitor in the village if talk went out that she had a lover.

'Will you come back here, then?' he asked.

'There's no work left for the next two weeks,' Visenuo answered. 'And we will be busy getting our house in order for the Harvest Festival.'

'Oh yes, the Harvest Festival! I had almost forgotten about that,' Atuonuo exclaimed.

'Isn't that when all the marriages that are

contracted in the year take place?' Kevi asked. It was more a statement than a question.

'That's right. All the marriages take place after the Harvest Festival is over. If you have your eyes on someone in your village, Kevi, you should think about taking them a proposal soon.' Visenuo could not have dropped a more direct hint.

'Then please do come back here. You can help me make a proposal to someone I like.' He looked from one woman to the other.

'Well, I am not sure when we can come again. We will probably have to use one afternoon to stack the straw away. But we will have to do that on a day when we are not observing the festival.' That was Visenuo's reply.

'And you don't think I should visit you in the village?' he asked.

Visenuo felt that she had not been very frank with him. There was an awkward silence before she answered.

'Kevi, as you can see, Atuonuo is a young woman now and she is considered to be of marriageable age by the older people of the village. She cannot be seen in the company of any young man. It would hurt her reputation, you see.'

'But what if ... what if I decided that I wanted to marry her?' Kevi asked with another of his smiles.

When he smiled like that, it was hard to tell if he was truly sincere or if it was all just a jest to him.

'Oh!' Atuonuo walked away from them in a huff. She really hated him at that moment. Was he so blind he could not see she cared for him? Let him be like that. She just might marry one of Vilhu's sons to get back at him and wipe that smile off his face, she thought. Her exasperation made her walk much faster than usual and the other two were running after her, calling out to her to wait.

When Kevi saw that she had no intention of stopping, he ran after her, catching up with some effort. He caught her wrist and begged forgiveness. She fought him all the way and would not look at him.

'I mean it Atuonuo, I mean it! I want to marry you!' he shouted in his attempt to make her calm down.

'I'll never marry you!' she shouted back. He looked at her even as he held her wrists.

'Do you mean that?' he asked in a much softer voice. Atuonuo was still angry with him and refused to relent. She bent her head and whispered yes. Then she grew defiant, lifted her head and repeated the word, loudly.

He dropped her hands as though they had burnt him. Only then did Atuonuo become alarmed by what was happening. She had never seen him angry before, but now she could see his face tighten with suppressed emotion. Without warning, he turned away and began running back the way they had come. Crossing Visenuo in his path, Kevi did not speak a word to her. He just kept running until they could no longer see him.

'Did you two fight? Why did he run off like that? Honestly Tuonuo, you could have acted more like a grown-up,' Visenuo began to admonish her.

'*He* should have acted more like a grown-up. He treats me like a young girl who amuses him. If he wants to marry me, he should treat me like an adult. Anyway, he is gone now. I doubt he will be back after that!'

'Come, my girl. We had better get home. Things happen for a good reason and if you are not destined to be together, it is better that you find out early than be hurt afterwards.' Atuonuo kept silent on the rest of the way home. She found that her anger had subsided, and she wondered if she had been too harsh with Kevi. She now felt silly for reacting the way she had. It was immature. She should have thought of a clever reply. Instead, she had acted like a petulant child and run off. Now she felt very embarrassed when she recalled her behaviour.

But Kevi had not behaved very well either, she

thought. He had teased her. However, she also realized that he must have been very hurt by her rejection, and she would never see him again now. There was such bleakness in the thought that she retreated from it. She would go home, she would forget she ever met him and direct all her energies into achieving that. Why did that thought make her want to cry?

It was easier said than done. That night, when she went to bed, Atuonuo could not sleep. She could hear her mother's regular breathing coming from her room. But sleep evaded her and all she could think of was Kevi's angry face just before he ran off from her. She tossed and turned, unable to get him out of her mind's eye. Every image that she conjured up of his smiling, beautiful face was blotted out by the memory of the face contorted in rage and hurt. She blamed herself completely for their falling out. If only she had had more control over her feelings. She loved him now, much more than she had loved him when they were exchanging sweet glances with their hands grazing against each other as she served him water.

When the first cockcrow sounded, she was still awake. Her eyes were red-rimmed from crying. She must get some sleep, she told herself, but it was hopeless. A thought came to her: maybe she could go back to the fields, and find him or leave a gift for him. Even if she did not find him, her gift would show that she still cared for him. That thought lulled her to sleep and she didn't wake until quite late.

'AZUO, I AM GOING TO THE FIELDS. I LEFT SOMETHING behind yesterday.'

'You can't go there alone. In any case, what did you leave behind that's so important that you have to go back for it today?'

'My hair band. It's my favourite one. I don't want to lose it and I'm sure it slipped from my hair back in the hut.'

'I can buy you a new one. Or we can go another day. Don't be in such a hurry.'

'No, I must.'

Knowing that her mother would never allow her to go alone, she headed to her cousin Aphreu's house to ask her to accompany her. Aphreu was Khonuo's daughter. The two girls were not particularly close, but they were family. When Atuonuo reached Khonuo's house, she was disappointed to find out that Aphreu had already left with friends to gather herbs. So Atuonuo was going back home dejectedly, but on the way she thought of telling her mother that she had been invited to gather herbs, and would be joining her friends in the forest. Her mother would not say no to that.

Visenuo readily allowed Atuonuo to go. This would be good for her, she thought. Especially after the turmoil of the previous day, she would be distracted by the company of people her own age. Who knew, she might even find out she liked one of the boys well enough to forget about Kevi.

So she was sent off with packed food and the admonition to be home before dark. As soon as she reached the forest area, Atuonuo ran all the way to their fields and slowed down as she neared the hut. There was no one there. She felt disappointed but went up to the hut, opened the door, and stepped inside. There was a powerful stench in the air. Perhaps she could expel it by making a fire, she thought. She bent down to start one when she heard a sound behind her. Before she could turn around, she found an arm holding her firmly around the neck. With his free hand, the man was holding her left arm and squeezing it so hard that his fingernails dug into her flesh. The pain was excruciating.

'Please let go,' she choked on the words. The arm around her neck was vise-like. 'Who is it? Please, please you are hurting me.'

'Are you hurting now? Are you?' the thick male voice taunted, and he tightened his grip.

'Kevi!' she cried out, 'I came to say I'm sorry. Forgive me, I don't know why I was behaving like that yesterday. Please stop hurting my arm, Kevi.' He didn't release his hold on her, and the pain was so acute that she went limp in her captor's arms and fainted away.

Now it was Kevi's turn to be terrified that he might have killed her. He picked her up and carried her to the bed. 'Don't die, Atuonuo, I'm so sorry. I didn't mean to hurt you.' Blood spurted out from the cuts on her arm where he had sunk in his nails. Hurriedly, he looked for rags to staunch the flow. He ripped the cloth on the bed to use as bandages for her arm. Then he looked for something to apply to her wounds. There was some rock-bee honey in a small bottle. There was very little left, it just about covered the bottom of the bottle. He put his finger into the bottle and got all the honey out, smeared her cuts with it, and bandaged her arm.

He kept vigil by her side, and after some time

she opened her eyes. But when she recognized where she was, there was a moment of pure terror. It all flashed back: the arm around her throat, and the nails pressing into her arm and hurting her so much that she passed out. She began to weep: big, heavy sobs that wracked her body and did nothing to ease her terror. Kevi reached around and held her and tried to comfort her. But his nearness distressed her even more. Finally, he left her crying on the bed and sat at a distance waiting for her to calm down.

'You hurt me,' she said accusingly.

'I'm sorry beloved, I thought I had lost you forever.'

'I came to find you,' she said.

'Why? Did you want to marry me after all?'

She looked at him intently but he was not teasing her. In all earnestness, he was asking if she wanted to marry him. And she said yes loud enough for him to hear.

'Oh my love, you make me so happy. How can you do both things at once? How can you hurt me so deeply one day and make me happy beyond belief the next?' He came to her and held her. This time she lay unprotesting.

'I must get back to the village,' she said after some time. 'Azuo doesn't know that I am here.'

'Oh, didn't you tell her? How did you manage

that?' The teasing tone was back in his voice but she didn't mind now.

'She thinks I am gathering herbs with girls and boys from my age group, but I ran all the way here to find you.'

'Oh my dear girl.' He held her hands and she saw that his eyes were moist. 'Atuonuo, will you promise me one thing?'

'What? Of course I will,' she said readily.

'Promise me you will always trust me no matter what anyone else will say.'

'That's easy. I love you,' she said.

'Promise me, then.'

'Yes of course, I promise. Now let me get home before my poor mother and the whole village finds out.'

'I'll take you home. It will be all right. We are getting married, and you are with your future husband. How can anyone talk about you when they know the facts?'

What he said sounded so right that she found herself agreeing with it. Atuonuo tried to get up from the bed and fell right back into it.

'Oh, why do I feel so weak?' she asked. She tried a second time and managed to get up, but the room swam around her.

'I'm so dizzy,' she said, and fainted again. When

she came to her senses it was pitch dark outside. She was alone in the hut. Fearfully, she looked around for Kevi but he was not there. Should she call out to him? The door had been left ajar. He would come back soon, she told herself, and then they would leave for the village. She would explain everything to her mother, beg forgiveness for having lied to her, and she would forgive her and be happy, too. Her mother was fond of Kevi and she had wanted them to marry, hadn't she?

'We can't go back tonight, my love,' Kevi said as he came in the door. He looked worried. 'There is a big storm headed this way. I could hear it when I went outside to check, and if we leave now, we will be caught in it. But we're safe inside. We must shelter here and leave tomorrow morning. I promise you I will take you back safely to Kija.'

Atuonuo became very anxious. If she didn't get back tonight, her mother would be worried for her. But the storm had already begun. The hut was being pelted by huge raindrops, and what sounded like hail. Indeed, they were hailstones that roared downward and exploded when they hit the tin roof. They could hear trees crashing. It was not safe at all outside for man or for beast. They huddled by the fire and argued over whether they should keep the fire burning.

'I could hold you and keep you warm,' Kevi said, but Atuonuo refused. So they pushed a big log into the fireplace and gazed at the flames even as the storm raged outside.

VISENUO FOUND OUT THAT ATUONUO HAD LIED TO her when she heard the voices of Aphreu and her friends returning home. It was twilight and their voices carried loudly across the square. She heard them laughing and bidding each other goodbye. Visenuo had finished cooking the evening meal. Any moment she expected her daughter to walk in through the door and tell her everything. After an hour had passed, she realized that Atuonuo had never gone anywhere with her cousin and their friends. It dawned on her that her daughter had, in all likelihood, gone to the fields to look for her hair band. Or for her beloved.

She made up her mind not to go to Aphreu's

house looking for her daughter. It would only create unnecessary gossip in the village, and tarnish Atuonuo's name. But now it was very late and she began to get worried. Of course Atuonuo was capable of looking after herself. She would never dare be out in the forest after dark, and she had never spent a night alone at the hut. But she wasn't alone. She couldn't be alone. She must have met Kevi and they must have made up, and quite likely he would bring her home even though late. Young lovers forget that their parents are sitting at home worrying. Visenuo comforted herself with all these thoughts. If Atuonuo and Kevi had decided they would marry each other, she would not be angry with her. She would refrain from scolding her. After all, it was so much more important that she find the love of her life, and marry him rather than become an old maid and look after her mother all her life.

The rain had come to the village too, with its deafening thunder and hailstones. There was no way they could make it through the storm to get home. She only hoped that they had stayed back at the hut. She would go as soon as the day dawned, and let the villagers think they had both spent the night at the hut.

But she could not sleep. One niggling thought came to steal her sleep away: What if Atuonuo were out there alone? Visenuo had no way of knowing if Kevi was there too. She got up and looked out her window. No one could safely make their way into the forest in that storm. *Oh let her be safe Kepenuopfu,* she prayed.

Mercifully, the rain came to a stop. Visenuo crept out of the village in the semi darkness and ran along the familiar path, carrying a staff for assurance and for safety. The way was slippery, and she slowed down to avoid a fall. The moonlight was watery and negligible, and she peered into the dark to discern the shapes of trees on either side of the well-worn path. It was slow going, but she had to be careful not to wander off in a completely different direction. The darkness was deceptive and the landmarks that were so familiar by day were no longer visible now.

The rain clouds had moved off and there was a little light falling into her pathway. Visenuo walked faster, her heart lifted somewhat by the weak light. Never before had she ventured out into the forest at such an early hour, and her heart trembled as she went further along the way. She had crossed the bend beyond the long stretch of fields that belonged to her neighbours. When she looked up, there was a dark figure up ahead. Was it some animal? She looked again while clutching the staff in her hand to use as a weapon if the animal should attack her.

Atuonuo came bursting out of the field path, her clothes bloodstained and her face tear-streaked.

'Azuo!' she cried before collapsing to the ground.

'Atuonuo! Are you all right? Are you hurt anywhere?' Visenuo leaned over her daughter, relief washing over her at finding her daughter seemingly safe, alive at least. She pulled her daughter to her feet and embraced her, but the next moment Atuonuo was pulling her arm, pure panic in her voice.

'We have to get away from here, Azuo. We have to get away from him!'

'What are you talking about? I'm here now. You are safe. I won't let anything harm you.'

'Azuo! You don't understand. We have to get away from Kevi. He is…he is *tekhumevi*!'

'What? Do you know what you just said?' Visenuo was shocked.

'Yes, I know what I just said because it's the truth. Azuo, please believe me! It's too dangerous to be here. He will come after me!'

Visenuò knew her daughter well. She had never seen her looking so desperately afraid before. She would do the questioning later. If Atuonuo was convinced Kevi was a were-tiger, she would take her word for it. They turned and ran together towards the village. But when they reached the boundary, Atuonuo said they had to go away from the village because that was the first place he would look for them. Besides, she added, everyone knew that the seer of their village was not powerful at all.

'Azuo, you don't know what horrors I have seen last night. We need to get to a very powerful village.'

'But where will we go?' Visenuo asked.

'Your father's village,' Atuonuo answered. 'Didn't you say that they have some of the best seers there?'

'Yes, they are very great. But it is at least a three-day journey. We won't be able to make it that far.'

'Then where can we go?' Atuonuo pleaded.

'We had best go to the Village of Seers. They can help us if no one else can.'

'How far is it to the Village of Seers?' Atuonuo asked her mother.

'I'm not sure.'

'Haven't you been there before?'

'I have. But it's different from other villages.'

'How?'

'The Village of Seers can be as far or as near as they want it to be. If you are a visitor they don't welcome, it becomes the furthest point on earth.'

'Is that why they call it the Village of Seers?' Atuonuo asked.

Visenuo did not reply but when they came to a crossing, she pulled Atuonuo onto a side path and they hurried along that way.

Visenuo still knew so little about what had happened back in the hut. The little bits of information that she had been able to get out of Atuonuo were that the two of them, Kevi and Atuonuo, had spent the night at the hut. Also that something unimaginable had occurred and Atuonuo was unable to tell her all the details. The one thing she repeated with much urgency was that Kevi had become a were-tiger and they needed to get as far away from him as possible.

MANY PEOPLE SUSPECTED THAT THE VILLAGE OF Seers moved location on a regular basis. Men got into endless arguments over its geographical location. While some swore it was five days' journey from Meriezou, there were those who were adamant that it was much closer, as close as a day-and-a-half walk away. The village of Meriezou was legendary among the Angamis; it was the seat of culture, the birthplace of many famed seers, and people still sought it out for answers. But the more adventurous and the needy travelled to the Village of Seers.

Men would crouch down on earthen floors, draw maps, and almost come to blows over what they thought was the exact location of the Village of Seers. Each man had a completely different idea of where the village stood. One man placed it very close to the borders of the Sumi villages. Another pushed it south of the country, and yet another located it in the heart of the Angami region.

What was the truth? No human could tell and it was pointless to try to situate it in a fixed location because it was inarguably the most powerful village, the village that held answers for all the problems that man could encounter in his physical existence. And by virtue of that power, the village was quite capable of shifting location as it pleased.

Visenuo took the road she had once taken when she had to consult a seer for her father's illness. He had been poisoned by his host at the village where he had travelled to conduct trade. It was a slow poison that produced paralysis. If no antidote was given, he would die when it reached his heart. Poisons used by different villages always had an antidote. The young Visenuo was sent to the Village of Seers because it was believed that the way to the village would open up without any trouble to a virgin. Anxiety had given Visenuo courage to make the journey and return. That was the only time she had been to the Village of Seers. She had not stayed more than an hour, only for as long as it was necessary for her to find the antidote.

And now she tried to remember all that she had

been taught about the village. 'Get to the great wood apple tree,' is what everyone had told her. That tree served as the only known landmark for the Village of Seers, a boundary between the natural and the supernatural.

'We have to find the great wood apple tree and then we will be safe,' she told her daughter.

They were continuing on the detour they had taken from the main road. The sun had risen high in the sky so they surmised that they must have been travelling all morning. With luck, they should be able to find the Village of Seers before dark.

They kept going on the little byway, which was sometimes so overgrown with grass that it made them doubt that they were on the right track. But at the end of it, the great wood apple tree loomed in front of them.

'Azuo, look!' Atuonuo shouted in relief. No one could mistake that gigantic tree, which stood at the gateway to the spiritual world, for any other. Its branches spread so wide that it could make a roof for five houses on either side. One could not see the top as it seemed to pierce the skies and disappear into the clouds. On the lower branches were ripe wood apples begging to be picked.

'Don't touch them. No one who picks the wood apples gets back home alive,' Visenuo whispered.

She looked for a trail that would take them forward in their journey, and a clear path appeared before them leading into the woods beyond.

'This way,' she said, and held her daughter's hand even as she navigated their passage along the track that alternated between swampy grassland and dark woodland. The total absence of insect and bird sounds heightened every other noise. A tree branch crashed to the ground like a felled colossus. The growling of big animals came very near them.

'Ignore everything you hear,' Visenuo warned Atuonuo. 'Just concentrate on reaching our destination.' As if to defy her warning, a cackle echoed through the trees and a flock of hornbills flew over their heads.

'We have to keep going,' she said, tugging at her daughter's hand again. Atuonuo's reaction was quite distressing. The sights and sounds of the swamp terrified her and she stayed rooted in her tracks, unable to move to save her life. Visenuo felt their progress slowed by her daughter's deep-seated fear. What other horrors would they have to confront before they reached the village?

Mercifully these strange sights ended when they caught up with two other travellers. It was a man and a woman, possibly his wife. The man's back was misshapen and he was hunched over, but the woman looked normal enough, and they nodded to one another, and exchanged the minimum of greetings as all of them hurried to their common destination, each immersed their own private nightmares.

SUDDENLY THEY WERE THERE, AT THE VILLAGE OF Seers, which looked commonplace, like any other village. The tall gate was made out of a single block of wood, and the carvings on it were no different than those on any other village gate. Figures of warriors adorned the front of the gate. There were four such figures here. Above and below the warrior figures were the rows of wealth and fertility symbols: female breasts, hornbills, the heads of enemies and mithun heads; shields and male ornaments like colourful headdresses. Many villages liked to carve spears and brew-horns, the ultimate male symbols, and the curious circles with a black dot in the middle. This gate was no different.

The wide wooden gate was open though it was

rapidly getting dark. The four travellers walked in together. Taking their cue from their fellow pilgrims, the two women stood beside them in the village square, waiting for a host to invite them home. An old woman came out of a house, and hastily pulled the mother and daughter aside.

'Better follow me before someone less human snatches you up.' She had addressed the two of them, and completely ignored the hunchback and his wife. Visenuo felt it would be impolite to wait for another host so they followed the old woman back to her hovel of a house. It was very old and parts of it was in disrepair. The lamplight from the kitchen showed the newly erected posts that were holding up the collapsed roof. But there were beds for travellers and the fire in the middle of the room was real and comforting. They sat down to warm themselves. Their hostess introduced herself:

'They call me Pfenuo. Let me warn you that it is not advisable to linger in the square after dark. Sooner or later a deceiver comes along and humans are no match for them.'

'What is that?' Atuonuo asked in alarm.

'Ah, deceivers will be found everywhere, but here in the village they crawl out of the crevices looking for fresh victims. There's only one way to determine whether a person is a spirit or a human:

Every human who comes here looks fearful and apprehensive, while a spirit appears peaceful and unperturbed by anything around it.'

'Thank you for rescuing us,' Visenuo began, but Pfueno brushed aside her thanks. She pushed back the strands of long grey hair that had fallen in front of her face and looked at them with all-penetrating eyes. It would be hard to tell a lie and hope to get away from eyes like that.

'What do you need from here?' she asked them directly.

Visenuo looked over at Atuonuo. 'Go on, you tell us everything that happened.' This was the first time since their long journey started that they could talk properly about what had happened. Atuonuo leaned forward a little. She first told Pfenuo a little about themselves and the circumstances in which they had met Kevi; his proposal of marriage and her rejection of it. She told her also about the regret she later felt.

'I went to the hut hoping to leave behind a gift for Kevi so he would know that I was sorry for my behaviour. I had no intention of staying behind. At first I saw no one when I entered the hut; suddenly, someone came from behind and held me around the neck, choking me. I couldn't move or shout. His other hand was holding down my left hand and his nails were piercing my skin. It was so painful that I fainted, and when I woke up Kevi was there asking me to forgive him. I wanted to return home as soon as we had patched things up, but I fainted a second time, and when I woke up, it was night and the storm came, and it seemed to last forever. Kevi said he would bring me home in the morning and that I should rest since I had lost blood and was feeling weak.

'We made some food and ate, and went to bed. He didn't want to keep the fire burning, but I said we always kept it burning on the nights we stayed at the hut, and I wouldn't let him put it out. I slept, but a little later, I woke up from the cold. By then, the fire had gone out. There was no sign of the storm that had blown with such fury. Very faint light from the moon was entering the hut through the cracks in the walls. And I heard the most fearful noises coming from outside. We were surrounded by tigers that were growling and circling the hut. My first thought was to wake Kevi up, but he was already awake. The tigers growled and scratched the walls, as though they were trying to enter the hut. It was dreadful! They got frustrated and growled angrily. Then Kevi started to growl back at them. He kept it up for a long time. I couldn't understand what he was doing. He growled loudly, almost as though he were scolding the tigers outside! Eventually they stopped their growling and slunk back to the forest. Except for the occasional yowl, we heard nothing more as they all retreated.

'Kevi laughed and said that was what his Apuo had taught him: how to speak to tigers in their own language. But I thought the whole thing was terrifying, though I didn't tell him so. He told me to go to sleep as they would not come back again. I feigned sleep but stayed wide awake. My heart was pounding with a ghastly suspicion. Could Kevi be one of them, you know, a *tekhumevi*? When he was growling, I had glanced back at him, and his mouth was wide open, and his teeth were long and pointed.

'I was very frightened but I tried to think about what to do next. I pretended to sleep and he fell fast asleep beside me. But whenever I moved he held me tight. I didn't know what to do. Finally, at one point, he was sleeping so soundly that his hand fell away. I saw that as my only chance and I crept to the door without making any noise. I looked back once: his face was completely covered with hair and he looked nothing like himself. I went out the door, carefully latched it without making a sound, and started running like mad. That's when you found me, Azuo.' Atuonuo's voice broke as she finished narrating her story, and she sobbed as though her heart would break.

Visenuo held her daughter and rocked her back and forth while Pfenuo stood by awkwardly.

'That's why you came here?' Pfenuo asked after some time.

'Yes. As Atuonuo said, he wanted to marry her and, possibly, she agreed to marry him yesterday...' Visenuo's voice trailed off.

'*Tekhumevimia*,' Pfenuo spoke up. 'They have immense power. Oh, I don't just mean physical powers but they have spiritual powers. I know there are many villages where their owners are consulted for their supernatural powers. We say they can *themou*, you know, predict the future. And you know how people like to hear about their own futures. The people who consult them are warriors, young men and also young women, rarely the elderly. There is a strong taboo surrounding the culture of *tekhumevimia*. Men want to take advantage of the spirit powers that the owners have accessed, so they are reluctant to kill them.'

'Are they men or are they tigers?' Visenuo asked.

'They are both,' Pfenuo answered. 'They have a foot each in both the worlds. So long as they are alive, they belong to the world of men, and the men that we call their owners grow more powerful and wealthy from this connection. But it is wrong to call them tiger-owners: the tiger and the man, they are one and the same. *When the tiger eats, the man eats*; we always say that. Some people insist that the man participates when the tiger is out hunting. We also say, *when the tiger dies, the man dies*. So they are very closely connected; they say the man is the body and the tiger is the soul. Some say they can interchange at will.'

'The right person for you to meet is the old seer. He knows what to do in these situations. We can go in the morning. Now you must eat something and rest. You are both exhausted.'

They ate a simple meal together. Visenuo thanked their hostess again, but Pfenuo stopped her as before.

'This is my life. The least I can do is to help those like you. Now try to sleep. We have to get out early if we are to meet the old seer. Day starts here before the first cockcrow,' she ended cryptically.

Though they expected to fall asleep instantly, sleep did not come so easily. That was because of the village. The square had come alive in the night. Visenuo and Atuonuo were glued to the window watching all that went on. Mooing cattle wandered around the square. Figures of men and women meeting and running from each other, barking dogs and long lines of women walking through the square carrying laden baskets—the activity was constant, and no one seemed to pay heed to the lateness of the hour.

After these had gone away, they heard ululating in the distance and, as they waited, a group of warriors appeared waving spears and prancing about in mock battle steps. While one line of warriors jumped forward with spears upheld as if to challenge an invisible foe, the other group went a step backward at the very same moment as if to avoid a spear thrust. It was a macabre dance executed very slowly.

Pfenuo returned to their room.

'None of that is real, mind you. Don't be deceived, and don't ever run out to watch. It's hard to save a human life when a spirit spear finds its target.'

With this warning fresh in their minds, they went back to bed. Atuonuo slept very soundly, but Visenuo woke several times in the night.

'GET UP, WE DON'T WANT TO MISS HIM!' PFENUO hissed as she stood over her sleeping guests. Visenuo woke up with a start and took some seconds to remember where she was. Atuonuo stirred but did not wake.

'Have you forgotten? Day starts here before cockcrow! If we miss him now, you will have to wait a whole week before he is ready to see you.' Visenuo scrambled out of bed. She shook Atuonuo awake, and found some water to wash her face. There was no time for tea and they left hurriedly for the old seer's house. They crossed the square which was now quite empty. But there were people on the streets, other humans who had also come in search of answers. They passed each other without a word, which Atuonuo found very odd. Back in the village, they greeted everyone that they met outside the house, whether they knew each other or not.

The old seer lived up a hill and the trio climbed a flight of rough steps that led directly to his house. The stone steps were uneven and if one lost one's footing, it would mean a fall that could end in a broken neck. They stepped carefully.

The door stood open. Pfenuo slid inside and the other two followed suit. The old seer was waiting for them.

'I thought you would come last night.' The way he said it made it sound as though it were a question.

'We are so sorry. It got late and my daughter was tired. So was I.' Visenuo offered.

'*Tekhumevimia* huh? A were-tiger makes for a complicated son-in-law,' the seer continued. 'But you should know that we don't kill *tekhumevimia* in this village.'

'What?' Visenuo was very surprised. She had expected some help in getting rid of the were-tiger permanently.

'You don't seem to understand the purpose of the Village of the Seers.' He looked at Visenuo with some irritation. 'We give life, not death. We give life to whomsoever and whatsoever desires to come into being. It would go against our principles if we were to take life. But humans, humans only know how to kill.'

'But that *tekhumevi* could have killed my daughter. He had his claws in her arm and was drawing blood that night.'

'True. But that still does not permit us to help you kill him. You should go to the woodsman if you want him killed. He is licensed by society to do that.'

'The woodsman? Is this true?'

'He is the only man who can help you against the were-tiger.'

This was quite a let-down. Visenuo could not conceal her disappointment, but Atuonuo stayed hopeful.

'Azuo, so long as we stay here we are safe, aren't we?' she asked.

'Yes, but we can't stay here forever.'

'And he cannot hunt us forever.'

Since there was no point in further discourse with the seer, they came back to Pfenuo's house. The Village of Seers looked very ordinary in daylight. People went about their work and the sounds of women pounding paddy and men chopping wood could be heard.

'They are real enough,' Pfenuo reassured them. 'I am not the only human in this village.'

'What brought you here?' Visenuo Pfenuo. They

had not had a proper conversation apart from the time when they had sat and listened to Atuonuo's story.

'The same as you. Oh it is so long ago and I have forgotten some of the details. But I came as a young girl, a bit younger than you.' She indicated Atuonuo. 'My grandmother had sent me because my uncle was dying. But he was a bad man. He had taken another man's wife and her husband had poisoned him. It's amazing the number of people who come here looking for an antidote for some poison or the other. My uncle was lying in bed, slowly dying from the poison.

'"Hurry," my grandmother said, "hurry back and if he lives, I will give you my biggest field."

'So I came here, not so much desiring to save my uncle's life, but goaded on by the thought of owning my grandmother's biggest field. She would give it to me, because she had said it in the hearing of the whole family. I was a young maid, a virgin, and that is why they sent me. Virgins find the way to the Village of Seers easily, as you yourselves know.

'I saw the same things as you did when you came here. I found the great wood apple tree, and followed the swamp road until it brought me here. But when I found myself here, something changed within me. I got the cure for my uncle easily enough, but I felt no desire to go back. You see, I had no one to go back to. My parents were dead, I lived with my grandmother who looked after me as a social obligation, but she only cared about her sons. I was useful as a servant girl, someone she could send out on errands. And apart from her I really had no family: no one who would care if I should suddenly fall down dead. The only thing that would sadden them would be that they had lost the person who ran their errands for them. I had no one who loved me. They complained that I was an extra mouth to feed, but every suitor who came for me was turned down because they didn't want to lose their errand girl.

"The Village of Seers is not the same for me as it is for you. You fear it, I don't. It is my home. I felt at home from the moment I stepped into it. I never went back with the antidote. I don't know if my grandmother found an antidote for the poison or not. I don't care to know. That life was never mine to live anyway. There are others like me here, not with the same story, but they all think of this village as home.'

Pfenuo's revelations were startling. The women were amazed, but now they could also better understand Pfenuo's place in the whole scheme of things.

'Are you happy here?' Visenuo asked.

'What is happiness?' Pfenuo scoffed. 'We know that word so little. The young fall in love but find fear and danger instead. The old have their aches and pains. I'm fearless now; I have surmounted both. I suppose you could call me happy.'

'STAY AS LONG AS YOU NEED TO,' PFENUO HAD told them. But they both knew they could not stay indefinitely. Unlike Pfenuo, they were not ready to give up the life they had in Kija, and become citizens of the Village of Seers. They were still too fond of the life they led, no matter that it could be hard sometimes.

The Village of Seers had its attractions though. Food did not seem to be a problem here. Pfenuo had an ample store, and would not hear of them paying for it.

'Do you know why the seers cannot kill the *tekhumevi*?' Pfenuo asked. 'It is because, after all, he is one of them.'

'How can that be?' Visenuo wanted to know.

'We knew Kevi and he was not a particularly wise man.'

'It is not about wisdom,' Pfenuo responded. 'It is the fact that he has crossed a line, and that crossing gives him access to the spiritual world. When they seek to become were-tigers they abandon their places in the human world. *The man becomes the tiger.* And we call them *tekhumevimia*. The crossing they make into the spirit world gives them the power to predict who will be victorious in war, and other such things. When they are consulted by relatives of a sick person, they can tell what was the particular spiritual cause of sickness in that person, and recommend a cure.

'For a person who voluntarily seeks to become a *tekhumevi*, the condition is a gift. But some men receive it as a legacy from their fathers. If such a man fights being a *tekhumevi*, it is a curse for him. Those who treat it as a gift make themselves available to more power.'

'How strange all this is,' Visenuo commented. 'Yet it also makes sense, because we say the same things in Kija, where we come from. Apuo used to say that the *tekhumevi* always follow the male line. If the grandfather was a *tekhumevi*, the son and the grandson would become were-tigers too.'

'Not only in the male line,' Pfenuo corrected

her, 'there have been some females who were *tekhumevimia*, but only very, very few. We knew a woman who was a *tekhumevi* in the village of Jumetou. She was quite beautiful, and sought after by many men. But she never married. I'm not sure if she is still around. If she is, she would be quite old.'

'I won't become a female *tekhumevi*, will I?' Atuonuo asked fearfully. 'He clawed me and I bled.'

'It doesn't happen like that.' Pfenuo chuckled. 'If you have eaten certain foods together, like chicken liver and country ginger, you could become a *tekhumevi* against your will. But you most certainly won't turn into one just because a *tekhumevi* attacked you.'

'Let's clean your wounds. We were too tired to do that last night.' Visenuo started to open the rags tied around Atuonuo's arm. In the meantime, Pfenuo brought them a basin of warm water to wash the wounds.

The blood had dried and the only marks left were four spots where his nails had punctured the skin and drawn blood. Visenuo cleaned the wounds while Pfenuo handed her some salve.

'These are claw marks, not fingernails! They've gone pretty deep. No wonder you bled so much!' Pfenuo exclaimed. She examined the injuries carefully and remarked that Atuonuo was lucky she had not lost more blood. 'We have to make very sure you don't get an infection. Let me put something on it.' Pfenuo went to fetch a bottle from the shelf and brought it back. She put the liquid on a piece of cloth and soaked Atuonuo's arm in it.

'That should take care of any infection. I'll get some clean cloth.' So saying, she went off to get clean rags.

'Oh Azuo, I never expected this,' Atuonuo said.

'Nor did any of us. And yet it is better that it has come out now so that we can deal with it. If we had not known, and if you had married him...!' Visenuo's eyes widened in horror. 'But we can put all that in the past and start afresh.'

'I loved him very much,' Atuonuo said in a small voice.

'I know my child, I know.'

She was weeping again, silently.

ATUONUO FELL ASLEEP WITH HER HEAD IN HER mother's lap. It was a mercy that she was able to rest after her long ordeal. Visenuo let her sleep as she herself dozed with her head leaning against the wall.

Afterwards, Pfenuo and Atuonuo watched as new arrivals streamed into the village. The square was filling up with several people, but there was no one whom they recognized. A man carrying a load walked past the square and disappeared into an alley. Two old men were sitting at the square but, Pfenuo assured them, they were both from the village. Pigs squealed as they were shooed off by every new visitor. They saw the old seer return to the village and walk right up the stone steps without a pause. Suddenly, a man walked into the square.

It was Kevi, as good-looking as ever, and peering in every direction as though he were searching for somebody.

'He's here!' Atuonuo cried in dismay.

'Who's here?' Pfenuo asked and came forward to look. She took in the tall figure at once, and the handsome features that were apparent even from a distance.

'That is Kevi?' she asked. Atuonuo nodded dumbly.

'Handsome fellow, let's at least give him that.'

'What will we do?' Atuonuo had turned deathly pale.

'What we will not do, my child, is to give in to our fears. You have to overcome your fear or it will be the death of you. Come and look at him.'

Atuonuo refused.

Pfenuo pulled her to the window. 'Look there. He is not a great hulking monster. If you don't let him, he cannot hurt you.'

'But whatever do you mean by that? He hurt me. He tried to strangle me and he made me bleed, and he made me so scared back in the hut.'

'So, make up your mind not to be so powerless the next time, because there will be a next time.'

'But he's followed us—me—here. And he's looking for me. What will I do?' Atuonuo wailed.

'Stop being afraid of him for once! No one is allowed to harm anyone in this village. He cannot do anything to you so long as you remain in the Village of Seers. But you can't go on hiding here. It's not what you want.'

'And I don't want to die,' Atuonuo sounded desperate.

'You won't die.' It was Pfenuo's turn to sound frustrated. 'What do you want, Tuonuo? What is it you really, desperately want? Come, tell me.'

'I want...' Atuonuo struggled to formulate her thoughts. 'I want, most of all, the life I had with my mother before we came to know Kevi.'

'It's not possible to go back into the past. You have to go forward. If you could have what you wanted, what would it be?'

'I want Kevi to forget he ever met me, and I want the same for me. I don't want him dead, but I want my life to be safe from him.' Simply saying those words out loud made her feel stronger.

'Tuonuo,' her mother called out as she hurried in from the outside. 'I have just seen Kevi standing in the square. He didn't see me.'

'I know, Azuo. Let's leave tonight.'

'Tonight? Are you sure? We are safe as long as we are here. Why risk going elsewhere?'

'I don't want to spend the rest of my life in this

village, nor do you, Azuo. We don't belong here. Let's go. We will be all right.'

'Why not wait until morning?' Visenuo asked.

'No. Atuonuo is right,' Pfenuo joined in. 'If you are going to leave, get a head start. I'll stall him as long as I can. One good thing is, he cannot leave this village as a tiger. If anyone tries to leave in a form other than that in which he entered, he can never leave the village. That will slow him down. Get ready, you two. No one will expect you to leave in the night.'

They had brought nothing so there was nothing to pack. Their hostess packed cooked food for them to carry on their journey.

'This could come in handy,' Pfenuo said, holding out a short-handled knife.

'I'll take that,' Atuonuo said.

They were soon ready to leave. They adjusted their body cloths—the wide, sturdily woven black shawls with red and green borders—to cover their faces. They carried a staff each, and could pass for a pair of old women.

'Thank you so much,' Visenuo said, standing at the door and looking back at Pfenuo.

'Nonsense. Anyone in my place would have done the same,' she answered. 'Now follow me closely,' she instructed as she led them out by another entrance to her house. They emerged at a section of the village that was quite deserted. The remnants of a stone fort stood guarding the village. At its base was a very low gateway which looked like a stile built to keep out pigs. Pfenuo indicated that they were to go through that. When they crawled into the dark, narrow space, and hauled themselves out at the other end, they discovered that they were very close to the swamp. After a few minutes of walking, the village was totally lost from view.

The night swallowed them up. The dark was a good friend and a bad enemy. They walked past the treacherous swamp, but nothing untoward happened, and they realized that the Village of Seers would not detain those whose spirits did not want to linger there.

They could recognize the great wood apple tree even in the dark. It stood hulking over the forest, darker than the darkness itself. But it was a happy sight for the travellers, a dear old friend. They did not dare rest, and they resumed their journey and soon came to the byway. They still kept off the main pathway but as the distance between them and the Village of Seers increased, they felt safer.

At first light, they found themselves at the crossing, the intersection of three roads. This presented a problem for them. If they continued directly ahead, they would end up at their ancestral village. The road to the left arched inward after a few metres and if they followed it, would eventually take them back to the Village of Seers. They didn't know what lay to the right of them, but since the other two roads were dead ends, they turned right and went on the third road. With any luck, the were-tiger would think they had headed back to their ancestral village and pursue them there; that would give them precious time.

They never slackened their pace. They constantly felt the urgency of getting further away from the were-tiger. If one slowed down, the other urged her on. There was to be no dawdling, no risks to be taken.

The road to the right was unfamiliar. The grass grew thickly in some places, as though people rarely used it. Around harvest time it was normal that the grass growth would decline dramatically until everything was as brown as the withered paddy stalks in the fields. But here the grass was still bristly and overgrown. They couldn't find a well-trodden path, and that made them wonder if they had taken the wrong route. But there had been no other way to choose from. So they continued.

Nobody came along the road. No houses or fields were in sight. They walked for miles without seeing any sign of human habitation. Day was far away, but at the edge of the forest a little light was beginning to trickle in from the sun loitering below the horizon. It lit up the path before them, and let them see that it was not totally unused, even though it looked deserted.

They kept to the grass-covered trail until they came to an abandoned shed. There was not much remaining of the original structure but a collapsed roof and three bamboo walls. The fourth wall was non-existent, and passers-by could see the interior of the house clearly.

'So, some people lived here once,' Visenuo remarked. Strangely it warmed their hearts to come upon the abandoned house. If they were to stop here, they would not get any real refuge. The rain would pelt them and the wind would probably blow over the remaining walls. Nevertheless, this shared symbol that meant so much to the human race had managed to touch their hearts too.

They hurried onwards without any sense of destination, unlike their journey to the Village of Seers where their eyes had earnestly looked out for landmarks, and their ears were cocked to catch every unusual sound. Now they were driven solely by the instinctive desire to live.

'My legs!' Visenuo sank to the ground. 'I've got an attack of cramps. Just wait a bit,' she said as she massaged her hardening calves.

'Azuo!' Atuonuo was very worried. 'What shall I do?'

'I'll be fine. Just wait for a bit; this rubbing will help me.'

After some time, the cramps went away and they resumed their flight.

'Tuonuo,' Visenuo began excitedly, 'I think I recognize this area. If we keep going we will find ourselves behind the fields and the forest, and then we will come to the woodsman's cottage! That is why we are on this road! *Kepenuopfu* has led us here.'

'Will we walk past our village too?' Atuonuo asked.

'Yes, yes. We will go past it too, but it is a very long way.'

'We'll find him, Azuo.'

They quickened their pace and tried to cover as much ground as they could while the light lasted.

The valley portions took the longest time to cover because there were no trees or rocks to hide behind. They risked long runs, slowing down at every big rock, and carefully looking behind to check if they were being followed.

Around noon, they heard the very welcome sound of an axe hitting a tree not too far away.

'The woodsman! It has to be him!' Atuonuo exclaimed.

'Wait, it might be some other person,' Visenuo cautioned. But Atuonuo was quite convinced it was him.

'It has to be Keyo. Remember when he visited us at the hut he said he had work beyond the village? This must be the area he meant!'

Sound carried easily in the outdoors. It was also true that a sound coming from very far away could seem very close by. So it was with the woodsman's wood chopping. He was far away, and they hurried as much as their strength permitted them.

'I'll call out to him,' Atuonuo said with great urgency.

'He won't hear you above the noise his axe is making. Save your strength for running.' So they kept running and the closer they got to the sound, the further it went away from them.

'Pray he will still be there for us,' Atuonuo said to her mother. It was deeply frustrating to have salvation so near and yet seemingly so out of reach.

They paused on the path and followed the chopping sounds deeper into the woods. Stop, listen, run, stop, listen, run again. That was how it went for the next hour until they reached the small clearing where he was lopping off branches from the tree he had cut down that day.

Suddenly, everything seemed to happen at once. At the same moment as they entered the clearing, the were-tiger sprang from the bushes and knocked Atuonuo to the ground. She screamed as she tried to fight off the animal, but she was no match for him. Her cries reached the woodsman. He abruptly stopped his work and turned in the direction of the scream, and could not believe what his eyes were seeing. A woman was being attacked by a tiger, and another woman was trying to fight it with her bare hands. Without a second thought, he ran towards them with his great axe outthrust. An ancient instinct told him that it was a were-tiger which was attacking the two women. He ran forward quite prepared to kill it. The tiger paid no attention to the woodsman as he continued to maul the woman lying on the ground in a foetal position with her hands covering her head.

The woodsman needed no more urging. He stood poised for the right moment to strike. When the tiger took another swing at his victim, the woodsman struck hard, with the accuracy of a hunter who knows there is no second chance. The blow was the mightiest he had ever struck. It cut the tiger's head in half, which rolled off the woman and landed on the ground, dead.

ATUONUO HAD FAINTED AND SHE WAS BLEEDING profusely. Visenuo was unharmed but badly shaken. Keyo recognized them at once and, understanding the gravity of the situation, said nothing.

He quickly picked up the unconscious woman and hurried off to his camp, telling her mother tersely to bring his axe. The woodsman laid the young woman on the bed and tried to staunch the blood flow from her wounds. He tore up a clean sheet and bandaged the worst of her wounds. The biggest cuts were on her arms because she had used them to shield her head. He bandaged each arm and put the right arm into a sling. That seemed to help.

Next he bathed her legs and neck which were covered with scratch marks. The bleeding from those areas was superficial. But she cried out when he lifted her a bit to check for more scratches.

'Oh that really hurts!' she said and opened her eyes.

'Where does it hurt most?' he asked.

'Here, where you held me when you tried to turn me over.' The fall had broken two of her ribs. She groaned in pain.

Just then her mother found her voice again: 'Tuonuo, Tuonuo, it's over. He's dead. He will never trouble you again.' The women held each other and wept for a long time. Keyo did not know what to say. When the weeping subsided, Visenuo tried to explain.

'Keyo, do you remember the young man you met at our field?' she asked. Keyo's brow furrowed for a moment, and then it cleared as he recalled the meeting.

'Atuonuo's young man. His name was Kevi, wasn't it? I remember him well, yes.'

Visenuo took a deep breath and spoke again:

'That tiger was Kevi. He was a *tekhumevi* and we didn't know.'

'No! To think I was chiding myself for my suspicions! When I heard who his father was, I prayed that he had not inherited it from his father. Who would have thought such a polite and handsome young man could be *tekhumevi*!

'Athi, Atuonuo, I'm so sorry for what you have had to go through I should have not stayed away so long. I should have confided in you about my misgivings.' He said remorsefully.

'No, it is over now. I thank *Kepenuopfu* it is all over,' Visenuo answered. She turned her attention back to her daughter, and carefully held her. She held her daughter close as she sat on the edge of the bed. In a little while, she would tell the woodsman the whole story.

Acknowledgements

I WANT TO PUT ON RECORD MY GRATITUDE TO Darrell Cocup who edited the manuscript of *Don't Run, My Love* with meticulous care. Thank you, Darrell for taking out time to give the grammar bugs a good bashing, and for going beyond the call of duty to get the manuscript shipshape. I owe you big time.